SONIC X

by Charlotte
Fullerton

Aqua Planet

Grosset & Dunlap

GROSSET & DUNLAP
Published by the Penguin Group
Penguin Group (USA) Inc., 375 Hudson Street, New York, New York 10014, U.S.A.
Penguin Group (Canada), 90 Eglinton Avenue East, Suite 700, Toronto, Ontario, Canada M4P 2Y3
(a division of Pearson Penguin Canada Inc.)
Penguin Books Ltd, 80 Strand, London WC2R ORL, England
Penguin Ireland, 25 St Stephen's Green, Dublin 2, Ireland
(a division of Penguin Books Ltd)
Penguin Group (Australia), 250 Camberwell Road, Camberwell, Victoria 3124, Australia
(a division of Pearson Australia Group Pty Ltd)
Penguin Books India Pvt Ltd, 11 Community Centre, Panchsheel Park, New Delhi - 110 017, India
Penguin Group (NZ), Cnr Airborne and Rosedale Roads, Albany, Auckland 1310, New Zealand
(a division of Pearson New Zealand Ltd)
Penguin Books (South Africa) (Pty) Ltd, 24 Sturdee Avenue, Rosebank, Johannesburg 2196, South Africa

Penguin Books Ltd, Registered Offices:
80 Strand, London WC2R ORL, England

Used under license by Penguin Young Readers Group. Published in 2006 by Grosset & Dunlap, a division of Penguin Young Readers Group, 345 Hudson Street, New York, New York 10014. GROSSET & DUNLAP is a trademark of Penguin Group (USA) Inc. Printed in the U.S.A.

Library of Congress Cataloging-in-Publication Data

Fullerton, Charlotte.
  Aqua planet / by Charlotte Fullerton.
    p. cm.
  Based on an episode of the television program Sonic X.
  ISBN 0-448-44254-X
  I. Sonic X (Television program) II. Title.
  PZ7.F9583Aqu 2006
                                                2005020457

10 9 8 7 6 5 4 3 2 1

Disappearing Into Space

Chris Thorndyke's schoolmates Linsey, Chuck, Danny, Francis, Nelson, and Helen all gathered around the teleporter in the lab at their school. The teleporter magically moves things from one place to another, and it had just sent their friend Chris somewhere! How were they going to get him back?

"Let's take turns keeping watch, in case Chris tries to send us a signal," Helen offered hopefully.

They had no choice but to wait and hope he was okay.

Meanwhile, Chris *was* okay. At that very moment, he was speeding through the vast

"When the Master Emerald pulses like that, it can mean only one thing," Knuckles explains

reaches of outer space on the spaceship Blue Typhoon. Also on board were his good friends Amy, Cream, Cosmo, Knuckles, Tails, and Sonic the Hedgehog. They were on a mission to retrieve all the powerful Chaos Emeralds that Sonic had thrown into space in order to keep them away from Dark Oak's evil grasp.

Tails sat in the pilot's seat, flying the ship. Everyone else gathered excitedly around Knuckles.

Chris said aloud what every one of them was wondering: "How will you know when there's a Chaos Emerald nearby?"

Knuckles explained, "The Master Emerald in the engine can sense the presence of Chaos Emeralds."

Down below in the Blue Typhoon's engine room, the Master Emerald was alternately dimming and glowing brightly.

"When the Master Emerald pulses like that, it can mean only one thing," Knuckles concluded.

A Planetary Surprise

"Are there any planets around here?" Amy asked Tails.

Tails pressed a button on his control panel. A three-dimensional star chart was suddenly projected onto the floor and slowly rotated.

Chris eagerly pointed at it. "Hey! Over there!"

"What's the name of that planet?" asked Cosmo.

Sonic had the answer. He was reading a guidebook all about the stars and planets.

Sonic pointed to a picture in his book. "It's called Aqua Planet."

Sonic imagined himself zooming all over the

landscape of Aqua Planet. Running super-fast was Sonic's favorite thing to do. And he always enjoyed going to new places to run for the first time.

Amy noticed the big smile on her friend Sonic's face.

"Okay, then," Amy commanded as if she were the ship's captain. "Head for Aqua Planet. Off we go!"

"I'm the captain of this ship, you know," Tails pouted. But he did as he was told.

The Blue Typhoon changed direction in space and headed toward Aqua Planet. The Master Emerald in the ship's engine room began to shine even brighter as Aqua Planet slowly came into view.

Tails piloted the Blue Typhoon down through the clouds of the planet's atmosphere. He prepared to land carefully on the surface.

"Um, why don't we call this off?" Sonic asked in an extremely worried tone of voice.

"Why chicken out now?" Knuckles teased him.

"I'm sure we've picked the wrong place," Sonic insists

Just moments ago, Sonic had been looking forward to this. What could have possibly changed his mind?

Tails looked at the view screen and saw *exactly* what was bothering his pal. "We're landing on water!" he announced. "And Sonic hates water!"

The Blue Typhoon splashed down, causing a huge wave.

Sonic showed his guidebook to Tails. The picture of Aqua Planet in the book clearly showed land.

"See? It's different from what's in the book!" Sonic insisted. "I'm sure we've picked the wrong place."

Tails began to sweat.

"No, we didn't!" Tails insisted. "I'm sure this is the right place! Something must have caused Aqua Planet's environment to change."

"I can't believe it!" Sonic cried. "No way!"

Everyone decided to get into individual mini-subs to explore the watery surface of

Aqua Planet, except for Sonic. Luckily, Chris had an idea. He welded two mini-subs together so Sonic could ride with him.

Aboard one of the single mini-subs, Tails gave the command, "Take off!"

All of the mini-subs, including Chris and Sonic's double sub, shot away from the Blue Typhoon like torpedoes.

Chris drives the double sub

Something's Fishy

Sonic and Chris's double mini-sub dove through the water.

Sonic gulped anxiously.

"I think I'm getting seasick!" he said.

Chris thought, *Sonic isn't at home in the water at all.* Then Chris said out loud into his end of the voice tube, "Don't worry. I'll take care of you."

Chris grabbed the control lever and made their sub speed up.

Just then, a mother sunfish and her baby crossed in front of the sub.

"We're going to collide!" Chris cried out.

"We're going to collide!"
Chris cried out

13

Chris steered the sub away in the nick of time and narrowly missed the mother and child sunfish. But this caused the double mini-sub to spin out of control.

Seasick, Sonic complained, "Hey! Give me a break!"

Meanwhile, Knuckles, Amy, Cream, Cheese, and Cosmo had already landed their mini-subs on a beach and were looking around.

"Is the Chaos Emerald really here?" asked Amy.

"No doubt about it," Knuckles replied confidently. "My intuition as a treasure hunter tells me so. Stand back!" He whipped out his shovel claw and dug into the sand.

"I guess I'll look somewhere else," Amy decided.

Cosmo remarked, "I wonder where Sonic and Chris are?"

Still out at sea, Chris and Sonic's double mini-sub came floating up to the surface. Their near miss with the sunfish had thrown them

"Hey! Give me a break!"
seasick Sonic complains

off course. The sub's canopy opened, and Chris and Sonic poked their heads out. Sonic was still feeling terribly seasick.

Chris spotted some land with a tall tower standing in its center. The tower looked like a lighthouse.

"Hey, it's an island!" Chris exclaimed.

"Huh?" Sonic felt almost too sick to look.

Chris docked the mini-sub onto the shore of the mysterious island.

By now, Sonic was way too weary to walk, so his friend Chris gave him a piggyback ride.

"See? It's land. You'll be fine now," Chris tried to encourage him.

"G-great," stammered Sonic.

Suddenly, some Metarex appeared! But they didn't look like regular Metarex. Their bodies were half-fish!

"Metarex!" Sonic yelped in surprise.

Chris supported his friend, who was unable to stand by himself. Now was sure not a good time for Sonic to be sick!

"What?" Chris replied, shocked. "You mean Aqua Planet has been conquered by Metarex?"

"Maybe its Planet Egg was stolen," Sonic guessed. "That's probably why it became a water-soaked planet."

Fighting Fish

The fighting-fish Metarex began their assault on Chris and poor seasick Sonic!

Sonic still managed to protect his friend Chris. He picked up one of the fishy Metarex and threw it. Then he punched and kicked some of the other attackers.

"Chris! Run for it!" Sonic yelled.

"What are you talking about? I may not look it, but I'm a black belt, you know," Chris said proudly. "Tanaka taught me karate! See?"

Chris took a karate chop at one of the half-fish Metarex. But partway through his swing, eighteen-year-old Chris suddenly turned into his twelve-year-old self!

That's what happened to Chris when his nerves got the best of him. **He shrank. And grew. And sometimes shrank again.** Now his arm couldn't reach his enemy. So he missed with a swish!

"Once more!" Chris said. He turned back into his eighteen-year-old self and set up to try again.

This time he kicked at one of the half-fish Metarex. But again, eighteen-year-old Chris turned into his twelve-year-old self. And his shorter leg missed.

"Quit playing around!" Sonic shouted. He kicked a Metarex half-fish.

"I'm not playing around!" Chris answered truthfully. "I can't help it."

Sonic punched two more attacking Metarex.

"Just go **hide yourself** someplace for now!" Sonic ordered. "And leave them to me!"

"Why?" Chris yelled, annoyed.

"Why?" grinned Sonic while pinning down a fishy Metarex. "You know. Because you're Chris!"

The half-fish Metarex
chase a shrunken Chris

Sonic still treats me like a kid, Chris said to himself. *My senses are just a bit off because my body shrank. But now I'm getting the hang of it.*

Just then, a fighting-fish Metarex attacked Chris!

"Take that!" Chris yelled, fighting back.

This time, Chris landed a punch. But the half-fish Metarex turned out to be made of steel! Chris's punching hand swelled up to twice its normal size.

"Ouch!" Chris hopped around in pain.

More half-fish Metarex attacked Chris.

"Chris!" Sonic called out.

A Metarex pounced on Chris. Sonic leaped to the rescue and saved his friend by pushing Chris into the sea!

"Whaaa!" Chris shouted as he fell into the water.

Now the fighting-fish Metarex stampeded toward Sonic! Sonic went into Tornado Attack Mode. He spun around superfast,

Chris's punching hand swells to twice its normal size

knocking away all the half-fish Metarex.

"Run for it!" yelled Sonic, returning to his normal state.

Chris headed for the safety of the sub. He looked back at Sonic and was shocked by what he saw.

"S-Sonic!" he screamed, frantically pointing, trying to get his friend to turn around.

A single fighting-fish Metarex, twice as big as all the others, loomed large behind Sonic! This was the Metarex boss.

The boss lifted a surprised Sonic high over his head. Then he threw Sonic into the sea.

"Ugh! Whaaa!" Sonic struggled in the water, trying not to sink. Sonic did not like the water one bit!

Chris started to go rescue Sonic but was startled by a crane suddenly coming from the lighthouse. The crane fired a net trap with a long wire attached, and the net covered Sonic, who was splashing in the water.

"Sonic!" cried Chris.

Sonic tries not to sink

The crane pulled the wire. The net, with Sonic trapped inside, was lifted high into the air!

The half-fish Metarex dove into the water. They swarmed toward Sonic, dangling in the net above.

Chris called out to Sonic, "I'll rescue you now!"

"Never mind me," Sonic shouted back. "Just get out of here! If you get caught, too, who's going to get help?"

"B-but . . ." Chris protested.

The swimming Metarex closed in on Chris's mini-sub. Just as they leaped at him, Chris slammed the hatch shut.

"I'll come rescue you somehow," Chris promised Sonic.

Underground
Secrets

Back on board the Blue Typhoon, Chris repaired the Hyper-Tornade as he filled Tails in on the situation. The Hyper-Tornade was one of the smaller ships kept on the Blue Typhoon.

"Sonic got caught?" Tails repeated, concerned.

"Yes. So I'm going to rescue him right now!" Chris said firmly, covered in grease, continuing his repair work.

"But do you know where to go?" questioned Tails.

"Not yet," Chris said. "But I'll figure it out."

Just then, a transmission came through to the Blue Typhoon. It was Amy's voice!

"Amy here. I'm in the basement of the island."

A basement? This was definitely not a normal island!

"We have some bad news," Tails said, "about Sonic."

"He got caught, right?" Amy said, not sounding surprised.

Tails was the surprised one. "How'd you find out?"

"The people of this planet told me," said Amy. She was surrounded by the original inhabitants of Aqua Planet!

Chris cut in. "I'm sorry. It's all my fault."

"Don't worry about it, Chris," Amy responded happily. "This gives me the perfect chance to prove to Sonic how much I love him by rescuing him!"

Tails and Chris listened uncomfortably as Amy acted out her pretend rescue scene.

"I've come to save you, Sonic," Amy said.

Then Amy imitated Sonic's voice. "Oh,

Amy, surrounded by the original inhabitants of Aqua Planet

thank you, Amy. I love you!" She even made lovey-dovey kissing sounds!

"Hey, Amy?" Chris interrupted.

"What, Sonic?" Amy said dreamily.

"Snap out of it! I'm Chris! Is there anything I can do to help?"

"Just don't get in my way!" Amy insisted. "And Tails, after I rescue Sonic, pick us up with the X-Tornade, okay?"

"Are you sure there's nothing for me to do, Tails?" said Chris. His face was covered with oil.

"Why don't you go take a shower?" Tails suggested.

The Hero Within

After Chris took a shower, he looked in the steamy mirror. He saw his twelve-year-old self in the reflection.

"I've grown so much these past six years."

Chris flashed back to starting college, studying karate, flying an airplane, and flipping burgers.

"I got to experience so many things," Chris complained, "but to Sonic and the others, I haven't changed at all."

Chris imagined Sonic, Knuckles, Amy, and Tails each fighting their various enemies.

"I don't have the tremendous powers

that Sonic and the others have. So I can't possibly do what they do."

Chris imagined Cream and Cheese flying through the air.

"I can't even do what Cream and Cheese can do!" Chris sighed. "Why did I come here?"

Chris lay on his back in bed, looking at the ceiling. He thought back to the exact moment when he decided to come to this world.

In his mind's eye, he saw himself looking around his old room. His gaze had stopped on a framed photo on his windowsill, a picture of him at age twelve with Sonic and his friends. A mysterious gust of wind had knocked the frame to the floor, cracking it. Chris had picked up the broken picture frame. A worried feeling had come over him.

Chris continued to lie on his back in bed, remembering these things.

"I sensed that danger was approaching Sonic," Chris recalled. "That's why I felt I had to come to rescue him."

Chris thinks back

Now, in his mind's eye, Chris pictured himself at eighteen sitting at an outdoor café with his college friend Helen. He was scribbling a blueprint on a napkin, coming up with new inventions that could help Sonic.

"What are you drawing on that napkin?" Helen wondered.

"A magnet barrier," Chris explained. "It can extract the energy of the ring from space."

"And this?"

"Speed shoes," Chris continued, "with special soles that increase the friction between them and the ground."

Helen smiled. "I'm sure they'll make Sonic very happy."

On the Blue Typhoon, Chris was still lying in bed. Suddenly, it hit him! He jumped to his feet.

"I've got no time to be brooding!" he scolded himself. "I'm not a kid anymore! I've got to do what I can!"

Helen watches Chris
scribbling on a napkin

Sonic was captured and needed his help. Even if Chris didn't have any superpowers like Sonic and the others, Chris did have his own special inventions.

So he went to his desk and got to work.

Operation: Rescue

Half-fish Metarex guarded the entrance to the Metarex base. Amy hid behind a rock. "So that's the place," she said to the Chief Magistrate of the planet, and all the other original inhabitants who had guided her to this spot.

"Yes," the Chief Magistrate nodded. "Please be careful, because they are not flesh and blood."

Amy understood. "They're robots." Then she charged at the half-fish Metarex, her hammer swinging!

Inside the Metarex base, in the Metarex

Sonic hangs off the end of the boss's fishing pole

boss's chamber, the boss was fishing, using Sonic as bait! A space shark flashed its sharp teeth at Sonic.

Sonic hung in the air, swinging back and forth at the end of the boss's fishing pole. "Hey, cool it!" Sonic shouted down to the hungry shark in the water below.

The space shark just gnashed its teeth.

While dangling from the Metarex boss's fishing rod, Sonic thought he heard Amy's voice call out, "Sonic!"

"Huh?" Sonic reacted, surprised.

Nearby, inside the Metarex base, Amy was using her hammer to clear a path for herself through the crowd of attacking half-fish Metarex.

She made her way up the spiral staircase that was against the wall, knocking over fighting-fish Metarex as she went along.

Back on the spaceship Blue Typhoon, the X-Tornade, which was another small craft kept aboard the ship, rose from the hangar. Tails was in the X-Tornade's cockpit.

The chute door of the Blue Typhoon opened. Tails entered the craft. The windshield of the cockpit closed.

"X-Tornade to the catapult!" announced Tails.

The catapult attached its hook to the X-Tornade's front wheels, then blasted it off the Blue Typhoon.

Chris, who was in his room working on an invention to help Sonic, looked out his window and saw the X-Tornade speed away.

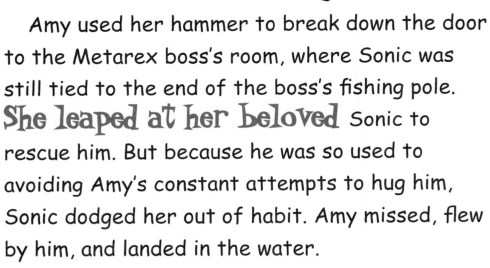

Saving
Sonic

Amy used her hammer to break down the door to the Metarex boss's room, where Sonic was still tied to the end of the boss's fishing pole. She leaped at her beloved Sonic to rescue him. But because he was so used to avoiding Amy's constant attempts to hug him, Sonic dodged her out of habit. Amy missed, flew by him, and landed in the water.

"What do you think you're doing?" a soggy Amy demanded.

"Sorry. Reflex." Sonic chuckled nervously, then suddenly shouted, "Hey! Look out behind you!"

The space shark was behind Amy!

Without even looking, she whacked it with her hammer. The shark fainted.

Amy jumped out of the water. She hammered at the half-fish Metarex and grabbed the fishing rod from the big Metarex boss with Sonic still hanging off the end!

"Sonic is mine!" Amy proclaimed.

She ran away with the fishing rod, dragging her beloved Sonic behind her.

"Hey, Amy! Be careful with the merchandise!" Sonic protested, skidding along the floor.

Amy ran down the spiral staircase, dragging Sonic. Half-fish Metarex closed in on them from above and below.

Sonic and Amy could hear the sound of the X-Tornade approaching.

Amy heard Tails shout her name.

She used her hammer to shatter the wall of the Metarex base. She burst outside, pulling Sonic along, landing right on the flying X-Tornade!

"Let's go to the Blue Typhoon for now," said Tails.

Amy carries the fishing rod with Sonic hanging from it

"First unhook me, will you?" Sonic said, pointing to the fishing rod. But there was no time for that now.

The X-Tornade flew away toward the sea. At the Metarex base, a whale gun aimed at the ship and fired several shots. But the X-Tornade dodged the attack.

"Oh, no!" Amy cried.

Tails wondered what was wrong, since he had just piloted them to safety.

One of the shots had cut Sonic's fishing line! Now Sonic was plummeting toward the water.

"That's why I said to unhook me first!" Sonic shouted up at them as he fell.

Water and Chaos

Just then, the Hyper-Tornade showed up, with Chris at the helm!

"Use this!" Chris shouted to Sonic as he fired a glittering capsule from the Hyper-Tornade. It made special shoes appear on Sonic's feet.

Sonic crashed into the sea. A huge wave rose. When it cleared, Sonic was standing on the water!

Amy called from the X-Tornade, "You're floating! How?"

Sonic beamed. "It's all thanks to Chris and these shoes!" Sonic was wearing hovercraft shoes that Chris had invented. Chris felt so proud. He had finally proven himself!

From the X-Tornade, Amy shouted, "The Metarex are back!"

The boss and the other half-fish Metarex swam toward Sonic.

"How dare you use me as bait!" Sonic yelled at them.

But thanks to Chris's hovercraft shoes, Sonic was able to fight back against the swimming, fishy Metarex.

The boss fired a large torpedo. It blew up near Sonic. The boss fired a beam. Sonic dodged it. The boss shot a spear from his hand. Sonic spun really fast and knocked it away. Now the boss himself charged at Sonic.

Sonic spun around faster and faster. Then he flung his spinning body into the attacking Metarex boss.

There was a gigantic explosion in the water.

Chris, Tails, and Amy watched anxiously from their two ships in the sky above.

The mist finally cleared. Sonic stood safely

on the surface of the sea at last. He looked up at his inventor friend.

"Thanks, Chris," Sonic grinned.

Chris smiled and nodded proudly.

Aboard the X-Tornade, hovering above the water, Amy noticed something like a beach ball floating on the sea below.

"What's that?" Amy wondered.

The beach ball sank. The water's surface sparkled.

"It's the Planet Egg!" Tails exclaimed.

The water began to dry up all around Aqua Planet. Land slowly became visible again. The planet's inhabitants cheered as the Chief Magistrate cried tears of joy.

Later, on the beach, Cosmo napped as Knuckles dug into a hill with his shovel claw. Cream and Cheese noticed a glittering blue light at the foot of the hill.

"Could it be a seashell?" Cream wondered.